# Catch an Echo

## This way

## Poems and drawings by
## Elliot Chester

"If you want your children to be intelligent,
read them fairy tales. If you want them
to be more intelligent, read them more
fairy tales." Albert Einstein

"Make it a rule never to give a child a book you
would not read yourself." George Bernard Shaw

"Write the book that wants to be written.
And if it's too difficult for grown-ups,
then write it for children." Madeleine L'Engle.

## Acknowledgements

Thom Phoenix Shaw, Leigh Stephenson
Rama Devi (Nina Marshall) proofreader, editor

## All rights reserved

# Contents

51. From Behind the Lines
52. Umbrella's not a Funny Fella
53. A Tale of the Beaufort Scale
54. Beware of the Stare!
55. What's a Housewarming Party?
56. Who's Driving Who?
57. Don't Shake your Head!
58. If One Should Squint their Eyes
59. I'll Have it Whole
60. Driven by Music
61. A Case of Furry Weather
62. Potato Panic
63. Unravel the Mummy
64. A Slow Downpour
65. Mrs Allergy has no Apology!
66. Oh, Where's the Voice?
67. It's Rather Cold!
68. A Sprinkle of What?
69. Dialling the Sun
70. Who's that a Knocking?
71. Mr Flexible
72. Emerican Anglish
73. Cheese if you Please?
74. Pins and Needles
75. You've got a Nerve!

# Catch an Echo

# THE LITTLE THINGS MATTER

A doll's house spoon, a speck of dust,
one coco pop, a paper clip,

a fish flake and a shard of rust,
a midget gem, one apple pip.

A sewing needle, piece of rye,
a toenail clipping, shred of skin,

a baby's tooth, a teddy's eye,
the crusty scab upon my shin.

A golden sequin, hedgehog's spike,
an eyelash from a neighbour's cat,

a sticker off a mountain bike,
the tag cut off from grandma's hat.

A pencil nib or some confetti,
a piece of fluff from 'tween my toes,

an inch of dad's uncooked spaghetti,
a thorn from mum's midsummer rose.

A sand grain or a toothbrush bristle,
a finch claw or a budgie's feather,

the ball inside an ancient whistle,
one lid to seal this box together!

A fairy wand, some frozen sap,
a ten pence piece, a strand of cress.

How many things can I entrap,
within this matchbox? Have a guess!

# TIE NUMBER ONE

My brother's tie collection
is varied and unique,

He always has to mention
that none must take a peek.

They should be in a circus,
and not around his neck;

they change their form on purpose,
then leave him in a wreck.

When he's outside, they're crazy-
one turned into a plane;

when one is deemed quite brainy,
you're soon declared insane.

It grew large wings and engine,
then swept him off his feet--

he got so much attention,
while flying through the street.

No tie is ever loyal,
they're stored away in closets,

and some are in the soil
where Bruno leaves deposits.

Some are in the pantry store,
in wardrobes, all for you.

And when you pick one from
this drawer--I'll write Tie number two!

# A SLOTHFUL CELEBRATION

Fifteen minutes to rub his eyes;
he'll look as good as new.

It takes one hour for him to rise,
then make the bed in two.

He pulls the curtains back at dawn;
it's noon before he'll eat.

I've never seen five minute yawns
or three to take a seat.

He'll never take a bath, incase
the water overflows.

The sloth will never pick up pace--
he'd rather pick his nose!

Today's the day that he will wed
a sloth just down the hill.

"They'll need a week", the vicar said,
"Who's gonna pay the bill?"

"She'll take her time upon the aisle;
he'll turn too late to view."

"I'll bet it takes another while
to say the words, 'I do?'"

"And guess how many hours he'll need
to lift her pretty veil?"

"A cheetah shows the need for speed.
They're slower than the snail!"

# CLOUD BUILDING

This catapult is always fair;
I found him in a dump.

He's one elastic strand of hair,
and stands on single stump.

I never fling what's hard or rough;
no stone or rock's his friend--

'cos all I launch is cotton wool,
to build new clouds on end.

# THE RED AND GREEN FLOATERS

Today, we'll do some apple bobbing--
an apple bobbing me.
And, through the woods, we'll go a robbing,
and shake loose every tree.
Today, we'll do some apple bobbing--
some fresh, and some with bruises.
And one will scream and start a sobbing,
if worms become intruders!
Today, we'll do some apple bobbing--
a hundred all afloat.
With open mouths and jaws a throbbing,
we'll count our wins. Then gloat.

## POLISH THE SLEDGE'S LEGS

I see the moon is full tonight.
I think it's made of snow.

I'll take my sledge to unknown
heights, and plant a flag, just so.

I'll soon end up on foreign ground,
whichever way I swerve.

Because the moon's not flat--
it's round--I'll fall straight off its curve!

# ON THE HUNT

O, why can't you cackle, Hyena, my
friend? Why can't you cackle real loud?
`Cos I'm rather funny, you'll ache from your
tummy, as laughter is always allowed!
I'll slip, and I'll slide, I'll tell a wee joke,
    then make you laugh till you cry!
I'll mix up my words, then frog like a
croak, then tickle your sadness goodbye.
Dear friends, my intention is not being
rude, I need a strong shot of Espresso.
I'd hunt for some coffee, before any
food. I'll laugh, but first, bring me Kenco!

# A SLIGHT INTERRUPTION

When fairies play on cello strings,
I sometimes hear off notes.
I'd rather see them splay their wings
in dazzling glitter coats.
I see them slide and twirl around;
they're sometimes rather cute.
They think they never make a sound.
One sleeps inside my flute!
They run upon piano keys
and ruin songs I play.
They'll never pay their fairy fees--
tomorrow or today!

## DID YOU MENTION QUESTIONS?

O, why does the moon never blink,
and why does the sun descend?

Why is the starlight baby pink,
and why does the rainbow bend?

O, why is a cloud now turning grey,
and what's the stratosphere?

Why do we spin throughout each day,
and not feel dizzy here?

# IS IT BIGGER THAN THE MOON?

How much will this balloon inflate?
I blow with all my might.
This purple orb of little weight
makes headline news tonight.

It's taller than the pyramids,
as wide as Ayer's rock.
I've never seen so many kids
all clasp their face in shock.

The aliens will soon inspect.
It's not a toy or prop.
Whoever's pricked, what bird has
pecked? I hear a massive pop!

# SHARK'S FIN ON THE HORIZON

I see a shark; can't sleep tonight.
it lurks within the skies.
Its fin's stuck out, a fearsome sight.
I rub my weary eyes.
And where's the moon to give me
power? The sun is still asleep.
It starts to sink within an hour;
through dreams, it starts to creep.
I never hear it make a sound.
I tell my mum and dad.
They say, "Tonight, the moon's not
round; it's crescent shaped." I'm glad!

## FANCY DRESS IS NO SUCCESS

Her outfit's wrong, she'll never win
this contest, fancy dress.
To their surprise, she marches in,
but who will she impress?
Her apron's tied, she's dusting stuff,
yet does not understand
that home's the rock, when waves are rough
and carpets are the sand.
"You haven't sung, no salty hair,
You've told no ancient tales;
The merman's on his own, right there,
he's looking for your scales!"
"There's some confusion, we all think
you're causing quite a stir."
"Stop cleaning rooms and bringing drinks--
and all you say is, Mer."

## LET THEM SLEEP

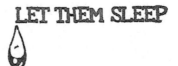

When dandelions fill the lawn,
they're in their summer glee.

If one should put near mouths, don't
yawn, just blow the fairies free.

They're in disguise, all huddled near,
high up among the grass.

Each dew drop is a fairy's tear,
'cos seasons come, then pass...

## COME OUT AT ONCE!

He'd squint both eyes and look

down slots, behind every TV.

He'd pick and poke, and shake 'til it broke,

then shine down a torch, just to see.

If people are really living inside,

then why don't they tap on the screen?

# WHEN FLOSS FILLS THE SKY

O, candy floss is everywhere,
it's everywhere we go.

These sugar clouds stick to our hair,
and cling to every toe.

And now, I've got some up mi snout,
I really need to sneeze.

There's no machine to spin it out?
It must be in the breeze!

# MR BUDDHA WON'T HARM YA!

I see a golden Buddha:
he's still, with upturned palm.

No shudda, wudda, cudda
is on his mind so calm.

Upon his feet, there's nothing warm,
no sandal, shoe, or sock.

He thinks that time's a useless form,
so disobeys the clock.

His eyes will never open--
this wise old chap from Delhi.

He'll charge no coin, or token,
for those that rub his belly!

# HOUSEHOLD FAIRIES

Monday's fairy has little fear
somersaulting in chandeliers.
He turns on the light;
this gives her a fright...
the glow in her wand disappears.

Tuesday's fairy is fond of the night,
a vampiress of pasty white,
one flicker of sun-
can never spell fun,
there's two cloves of garlic in sight!

Wednesday's fairy is sporty and free;
he loves to swim in cups of tea
the silver spoon stirs.
A whirlpool occurs;
he ignored the forecast, you see.

Thursday's fairy sleeps in thimbles
painted gold in pretty symbols
he pinches all snacks,
leaving telltale tracks-
the fairy life's oh so simple!

Friday's fairy flits around eyes,
slides down a lash, then says goodbyes,
her life's on the brink,
whenever you blink,
'cos nobody hears when she cries.

Saturday's fairy's overweight,
a buddha belly--always late;
his wand can't uphold
a waistline so bold--
topheavy and can't stand up straight.

Sunday's fairy is rather sly;
she falls between a needle's eye
but swings on a thread
'cos her wings play dead.
She'll get sewn in a shirt, oh my!

This outing now comes to a close;
though one still slides upon his nose,
it's time for farewell,
now leave where they dwell.
They'll return at the wag of your toes.

## BENEATH THE MAGIC ROLLING PIN

My grandma used to always say,

whenever one begins to doubt:

just make some dough then press away,

To dim all thoughts that tap, then shout.

And 'neath the magic rolling pin,

your troubles start to flatten.

Roll back and forth to stretch its skin--

you'll see no marks, no pattern!

# I'VE BEEN A SILLY BILLY!

Just what have I put my foot in?
I really am confused!
Is it Auntie Carol's pudding
while wearing mummy's shoes?
Is it deep in soil and smelly,
or through the moon of cheese?
is it stuck within a welly,
or in a hive of bees?
Is it safe to bring the other
and cause a spot of grief?
I should stay beneath this cover,
but hiding will be brief.
Is it stuck within the trifle,
and looking oh so sweet?
It really is an eyeful,
this poem caused by feet.
But it's just one, not two, not three;
I'll not involve its mate.
I may have dropped the vase, you see,
or stood on grandma's plate.
Next time, I'll dip one toe in,
then quickly pull it out;
then surely no one's knowing

of what may come about...
Is it stuck within some quicksand,
or concrete just been spilt?
And why's it foot, and never hand?
And will it bend, or tilt?
I guess I'm in some trouble.
That phrase has just been said.
Their phone bill's nearly double...
they've turned a shade of red!

# MARY MARINE'S DEN

A short rhyme from staff at Mary Marine's Den,
our whimsical menu inspires a poet's pen...

Welcome to our den of excellent cuisine
where fantasy rids your stresses and
troubles, found undersea, by Mary Marine;
mermaids take orders enclosed in bubbles.

Seahorses sing you anthems of the ocean
and hang your jackets on a swordfish's nose;
laughing lobsters pour you a potion, that's
just a taster to keep you on your toes.

## Appetisers (thirty fairy emerald coins)

Tomato soup with a cream stardust muse
(Delivered by shooting stars)

Charming caviar with soft moonbeam centres
(Top review from cosmos)

Fruit tartlet topped with humming Banana skins
(Don't let this one slip)

## Main (fifty pixie pennies)

# menu

Beans and cabbage pie served by flatulent fairies
(Nose pincher)

A supreme chicken pizza and a disco lights crust
(Loved by Diana Ross)

Clapping Oysters served with seaweed crust
(A holistic must)

## Desserts (forty wise old wizard coins)

Apple crumble pie served by a skating bookmark
(Every need for speed)

Medusa's hissing ice-cream sent on a
charmed snake, (It's rude to stare)

Orange Mousse with caramelised fairy dust
(Tinkerbell on overtime)

Thank you for dining at Mary Marine's Den;
we will excite you with magic, again and again.

## SHUTTLECOCK BOY


His clothing is a plastic mesh,


a rubber mask, his face.


And when he greets the racket--


his flying picks up pace.

# I WATCH THE WINGS

I waft my arms like hummingbird's wings;
they're so much tinier than I.

But feathers weigh much less than limbs;
they compliment the sky.

If I was a hummingbird, hummingbird.
If I was a hummingbird in a pinkish sky,

I'd take a swoop at bursting berries,
as all my roads are made of air.

I'd dart past fishermen in their wellies,
and never stress of wind blown hair.

If I was a hummingbird, hummingbird.
If I was a hummingbird in a pinkish sky.

## I'VE GONE CRACKERS!

My eyes are rainbows, my nose a Sahara dune,

the stars are my freckles; each one hums in tune.

My smile is a stream with teeth as white lilies.

Cheese before bed makes my dreams go all sillies!

# MR TRICKSTER STRIKES AGAIN

"Erm...Edward can't come in today,
I'm afraid he's got the flu."
The chickenpox have come to play
he's spewed up last night's stew."

"He's sweating like Niagara falls
and moving so robotic."
He hasn't seen outside these walls.
It's turning him psychotic."

"He's got the mumps, contagious,
his temperature has soared.
Can't even tie his shoelaces,
he should be on a ward!

"He's turning cold like arctic slab,
the bin is full of drool.
More potions than a science lab,
his bed has gained a stool."

*'I know it's Edward on the phone,*
*Your father's just drove past!"*
"Erm, I can't drive, I have a clone;
my leg's still in a cast!"

"He hasn't touched his cereal,
his homework's not been done."
*"Your skiving school's illegal;*
*now still your fibbing tongue!"*

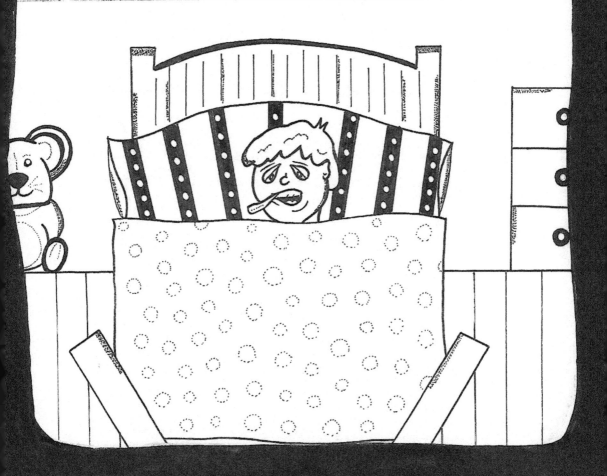

# SIZE 3000 PLEASE?

My feet are very long and wide,
they block the rays from sun.

I cover miles in just one stride,
and each one weighs a tonne.

When I lay down, I feel the snow
way up the mountain range.

And every tip of every toe
will feel the weather change.

I need a thousand yards of lace
to tie each shoe with knots of nine.

I can't compete in any race--
before we run, they cross the line!

# VENDING DELIGHTS

The fairy folk replace all snacks--
no gum, cola, or sweet.

They've flown through every hole
and crack, but none are safe to eat.

The latest craze: some pink, some
blue, and some with chocolate gown.

Some cost a token, maybe two--
they'll never ever frown.

I see their frocks for sale in packs,
with tubes of golden dust.

The young ones carry gems in sacks;
the old ones gather rust.

I see a battery charging kit
for sale on level three.

# MUNCHIES

They're full of charm and
cosmic wit, but never fall for free.

Behind each spiral, silver bright,
they're pushed towards the end.

At times, it gets a little tight;
a sign goes up: 'Please Mend.'

Just give soft nudge, with open palm,
your purchase will drop south.

These fairy folk will cause no harm.
They're real. Now close your mouth!

# MR CELLOTAPE

Mr cellotape will never grin.
He doesn't like the snip.
He's rather mean. He'll pull
the skin off anybody's lip.

And when he's folded at the ends,
he's easier to use.
He likes it when his haircut blends,
and gives no hints or clues.

A greasy print can bother him.
He's dizzy when he's rolled.
At Christmas time, he'll get quite thin,
and start to feel the cold!

# THEY COME TO LIGHT AT NIGHT

I wonder why they're called cat's eyes
upon the UK's roads?
And do they blink while in disguise,
and do they meow their codes?
They must get bored of staring, so,
they never seem to move.
Who trims their whiskers as they grow?
What are they trying to prove?
And where's their bodies...underneath,
who feeds them while they glow?
I've never seen their feline teeth
or shine beyond the snow.
The ground's just shook, a purring cat,
it must be getting freed?
An exit's through the roadside flap,
but there's no need for speed!
I wonder if their backs will arch
when seeing things in fright?
What happens when the doggies bark?
I wonder if they bite?

# I SEEK THE MOON'S DELIGHTS

I need to entertain these crowds;
I seek a new pinata.
Upon these stilts, I walk through clouds;
they're really hard to master.

I'll pluck the moon and bring it down
and hang it from an Evergreen,
Then watch it light up all the town;
the biggest light bulb ever seen.

We'll hit, until it spills its gold,
with rods and sticks and chains and whips.
We'll tell the sun it got real old,
then disappeared. A rare eclipse.

# FILL THE WORLD

The Earth is hollow as a tennis ball,

it needs to be cut in two.

Each half should be crammed

with love and laughter.

Then put back together with glue.

# MR MAGNET THE GIANT

All metal gives him energy,
this everybody knows.

He loves to wear all cutlery
and coins on tips of toes.

There's two car doors from scrap
heap piles, now stuck upon each palm.

An aeroplane is pulled for miles--
the landing strip's his arm.

A candlestick upon his head,
some screws and nails on brows.

And, on each shoulder, slabs of lead,
and round his neck, the bells of cows.

A silver bolt like Frankenstein,
two dungeon balls swing from his hips.

A garden fork against his spine,
and on his chin, six paper clips.

He's not a fan when lightning strikes;
he'll hide behind a rock.

Around his ears are wheels of bikes,
and on his nose, a clock.

If one should see him, walk away.
This giant's no cool geezer.

He's after kitchen parts today--
he wants your fridge and freezer!

# I WATCH THE CLOUD'S FORMATIONS

I look among the clouds again.
with squinting eyes, I see
an army of a dozen men
and a weeping willow tree.

I see a chain of daisies bright,
which come apart too soon.
A hand is reaching for its kite,
but soars beyond the moon.

I see the peaks of Austria,
which flatten to a lake.
I scan a mystic warrior,
and seven tiers of cake.

And when they're grey and full
of loss, I'll never beg their pardon.
I see the clouds as whitened moss--
a glimpse of heaven's garden.

## MEMBERS OF THE MOON

I'm riding the carousel on the moon's halo.

Spinning and spinning, it turns without coin.

Horses like Pegasus, with wings all aglow--

If one should believe, you're welcome to join.

# NO CATAPULT TO SEND YOU FLYING!

My friend: the moon's not a light to escape.

It's not a large hole in the sky.

So, leave your telescope and plastic cape--

you don't even know how to fly!

# CATCH AN ECHO

I've shouted from the hills to see
if echoes can be caught.
But all they do is times by three
then disappear to nought.

I've seen them bounce off walls
in caves, and shatter panes of glass.
I've heard that whales beneath the
waves attend a sonar class.

I'd catch the notes that I once sang—
there's now one in my reach!
An echo's like a boomerang.
And this is what I'll teach.

# SERPENT'S MEAL

I think that's a snake, not a garden hose,
all coiled up nicely and tight.

It looks fast asleep, or charmed,
I suppose--or just made of plastic, right?

Try and unwind, then screw to a tap;
if one hears a hiss, then it's real.

But I'd rather not be wiped off the map
and doomed for a serpent's meal!

# IT'S NOT A CROAKING MATTER

"It's toad in the hole for tea," mum said.
But how is she going to catch it?
And is it alive, or will it be dead,
and are they for sale at the market?

Now, I'm confused, it sounds rather mean;
just where is this hole that it goes in?
And do they remain all slimy and green,
and are they cooked fresh, or from frozen?

And will they use frogs, they ribbit too,
and are they caught with a cage and net?
It's sausages cooked in a pudding, it's true.
There's no need to hide your favourite pet!

# I'LL PUT THE SPRING IN YOU

O, why's this onion called a spring?
Does it bounce or have a coil?
Does it somersault, then start to sing
when freed from beds of soil?

I've seen their heads are upside down,
with legs up in the air.
And when they're shipped away
from town, who cuts their wiry hair?

Do scarecrows scatter all the pips,
will mummy cry when slicing?
It's every March they'll show their tips--
preparing for their pricing.

# HOW DO THEY GALLOP?

I've never heard a sea horse neigh
or seen a mane or hoof.

I've never seen them eating hay
below the water's roof.

I've never seen them open jaws
to show discoloured teeth.

I've never seen them fight in wars
behind the coral reef.

I've never seen them used as slaves
to carry every fish.

I've never seen them leap through waves,
although it's what they wish.

I've never seen them balancing;
they really cannot swim.

I've never heard them challenging
the fact they have no limb.

I've never seen them move with force,
their diet's never grass.

"They're not related to the horse,"
the teacher tells the class!

I've got one more to add before,
and then, I'll sit, I swear.

Why's the sea lion never roar,
and where's its orange hair?

# MRS COMPASS NEEDS A REST

She pirouettes and leaves a trail
and illustrates the sphere.
Sometimes, one leg is rather frail,
but never sheds a tear.
At times, it's left, at times, it's right;
the pencil keeps her steady.
She'll rip the page when pushed
too tight; that means she's not quite ready.
Some days, she'll speed, some days,
she's slow, but needs a helping hand.
And when her head is pressed,
she'll know her feet are in demand.

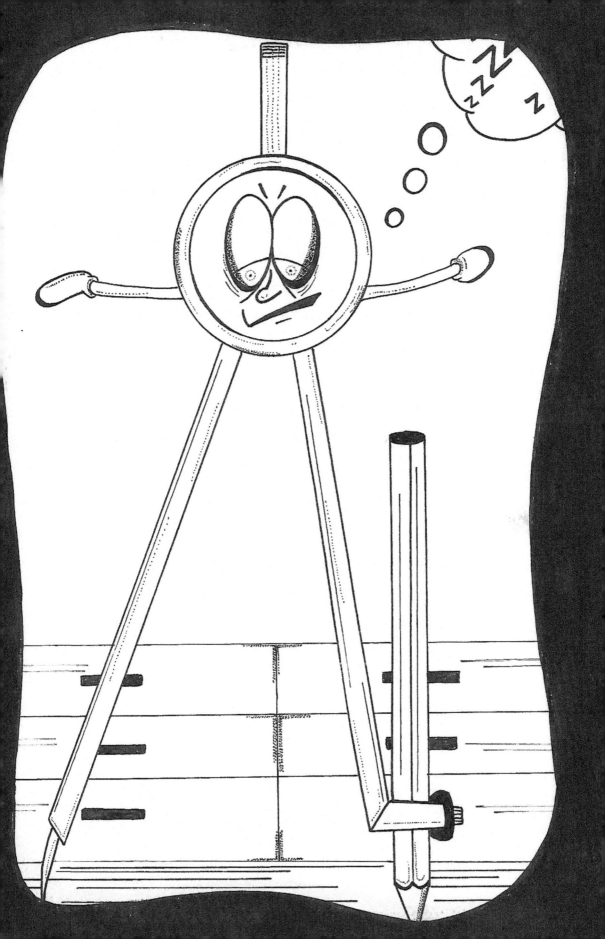

# MISHMASH PAELLA

I know paella's made of rice,
it's tossed within a pan,
with vegetables and flavoured
spice. I'll add just what I can.

But are there any stoppages,
to what goes in the mix?
I compliment the sausages
with crumpled weetabix.

Some pastry from a quiche lorraine,
one slice of cheese (including mould)
And now, there's some torrential
rain, of chilli powder, six years old.

I'll add a bunch of stale sardines
and popcorn off the floor.
The juice from sour nectarines,
a dozen meatballs, raw.

I crack four eggs and stir it well,
there's fly infested margarine; to mix
into this dish of hell, two
squashed tomatoes, one baked bean.

I double check to see who's looking.
Some stinky kippers, heaps of salt.
One lozenge that I've just been sucking.
And zero cares, it's all my fault.

And now, I get some cravings,
ten olives stuffed with dirt and fluff.
Some chewing gum from public pavings,
but surely that just ain't enough?

Some ketchup mixed with mayonnaise,
ten spoons of coffee, add some drool.
I hope this dish receives some praise,
and gets on plates in every school!

# WHAT GOES ON UP THERE?

Where do gods and goddesses live,
as all I see is empty sky?
Do they shake the stars from heaven's
sieve, and bake eternal pie?

Do they float or walk on wooden boards?
Will they eat banana split?
And are they armed with shields and
swords? And do they stand or sit?

Are cherubs perched within the crowd?
Are mirrors there to pose?
And do they hide behind each cloud
when trying on new clothes?

# IF ONLY THEY KNEW!

She never holds her mouth or nose
whenever she achoos.

Her tissues never feel the blows,
and all she'll hear is boos.

The people run, escape on bikes;
her sneezing will disgust.

One gasp of breath--and now it strikes--
she sneezes fairy dust!

# MR TING LIKES THE WIND

A simple note, unlike the gong,
drowned out by cello strings.

The triangle is very strong,
although he only tings.

The woodwind lot are better
known; he's not a fan of bass.

He likes the sound of nature's tone,
when wind blows through his face.

# CATCH OF THE NIGHT

It hangs upon a drawing pin,
so dreams can form a queue.
Then throws all nightmares in the bin,
but lets the good stuff through.
For demons lurking on the roof,
you're not the welcome crowd.
It lets the fairy claim a tooth,
but ogre's aren't allowed.
The gemstone feathers hang and
waft, no spider's in the web.
No threads will feel a monster's
draft, no forehead starts to sweat.
I hope my sheets are washable,
I dreamt of gushing taps.
The yellow flows unstoppable,
I wet the bed, perhaps!

# A GLOBAL WARNING

I know my freezer's big enough
to stack each iceberg high.

There's plenty room for arctic
stuff; I'll even fit the sky.

And then, I'll set the sun
on top, to never overheat.

No ocean levels rise, or drop.
No worries what to eat.

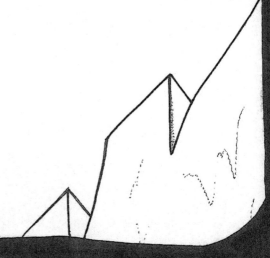

## KEEP DECAY AT BAY

Oi! put that can of coke away,
your teeth will start to rot;

no fairy will attend and pay,
if yellows all they've got.

Instead of lifting pillows back
in upset and despair--

all teeth remember what they lack-
and that, my friend, is care!

# I'LL GET IT OUT OF YOU

What's in the bag? Oh, please explain.
I really wanna know.
Ten hot cross buns, a phantom pain,
or heaps of yellow snow?
A cosmic pie, old cutlery,
a rainbow in a knot?
Or Jupiter, a memory
that came and since forgot?
A dirty bathtub full of suds,
imaginary friend?
A heap of junk, unwanted goods,
a bar that doesn't bend?
A boomerang that wants to fly
or bric-a-brac, ker-plunk?
A penny, but without the guy--
the smell without the skunk?

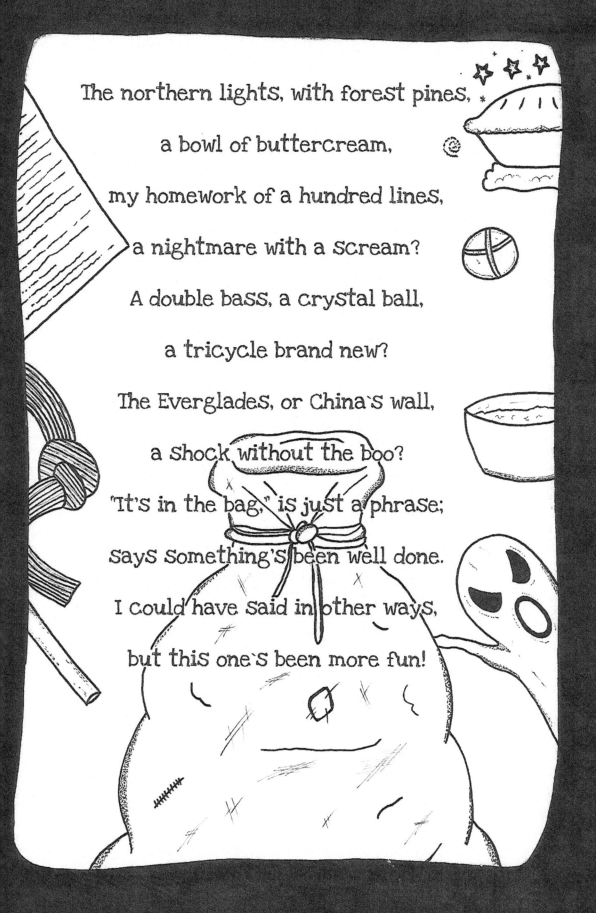

The northern lights, with forest pines,

a bowl of buttercream,

my homework of a hundred lines,

a nightmare with a scream?

A double bass, a crystal ball,

a tricycle brand new?

The Everglades, or China's wall,

a shock without the boo?

'It's in the bag,' is just a phrase;

says something's been well done.

I could have said in other ways,

but this one's been more fun!

# ST. PETERSBURG OR MOSCOW?

Around my waist, I see no mark;
of that I'm glad, you see.
I can't remove my upper half
to find a smaller me.
I wonder if I've got some more
that live beneath my skin?
They're maybe five, or even four--
but are they large, or thin?
And do they share the air I take,
all trapped in spaces small?
The Russian dolls must need a break,
from standing still, and tall.
Who's moody, quiet, funny, grim?
Who's elegant, or sick?
Not sure who's who, or her, or him,
or what makes others tick.
One taps on two, two taps on three,
three taps on four, and so.
And now, my hands must lift them free--
I wonder where they'll go?

# HE HANGS THE UNIVERSE OUT TO DRY

He wants to clean all outer space,
our universe must stink.

He catches planets in a case
then scrubs them in the sink.

No brillo, brush or elbow grease
compares to the washer.

And now the iron kills each crease--
they've never looked as posher!

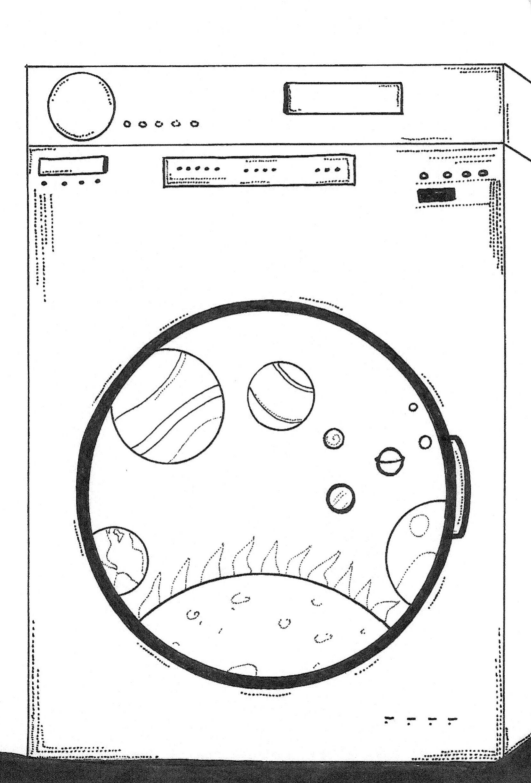

# FROM BEHIND THE LINES

This group of clefs take on new form,

they rise and fall through streets.

They fly thorugh skies, through sun,

through storm, now freed from music sheets.

# UMBRELLA'S NOT A FUNNY FELLA

I spot a seagull in mid-flight,
circling the Brighton air.

A different kind of rain's in sight;
but brolly doesn't care.

My forehead has befriended poop;
Oh, get me in the bath!

Not sure if it was stew or soup?
It opens up to laugh!

# A TALE OF THE BEAUFORT SCALE

I've heard of Mrs Beaufort scale;
She loves to entertain.
At times, she'll blow a heavy gale
and disarrange the rain.

Though one to two is very mild,
a pleasant breeze is felt.
Not strong enough to push
a child, nor nudge Orion's belt.

She'll change the way that smoke
will rise, then rubbish starts to soar.
And people know that when she
sighs, it's gone from three to four.

She loves to fill the trees with dread
and free its leaves and sticks.
And when the hats blow off each head,
you know it's five to six.

It's seven, eight, can't stand upright;
she starts to cough, then wheeze.
The cars are shaking, what a sight!
It's calmer than her sneeze.

It's nine to ten, there's flying bins.
(No blade of grass, or tuft?)
It's fair to say that Beaufort wins
when cheeks are fully puffed.

HELP!

At eleven or twelve, people fly,
no roofing's left at home.
As nature needs no alibi,
she blows the seas to foam.

No numbers left, the windows crack--
there's chaos everywhere!
It's hard to write upon my back--
while whizzing through the air!

# BEWARE OF THE STARE!

It's in Peru or Chinatown,
beside Gibraltar's rock.
It's underneath the eiderdown,
or crumpled in a sock.
It's mailed in space with satellite,
with no 'return-to-sender.
It stumbled on some dynamite.
or spinning in the blender.
I think I steamrolled by mistake:
it's flattened in the path.
It's now a paper mache cake,
or soaking in the bath.
I simply saw it disappear,
it must be lost in transit.
But homework isn't needed here,
the teacher said she's banned it!
I've heard that there's a costly fine.
I've made a few excuses.
I'll see the head, then stand in line--
her eyes are like Medusa's!

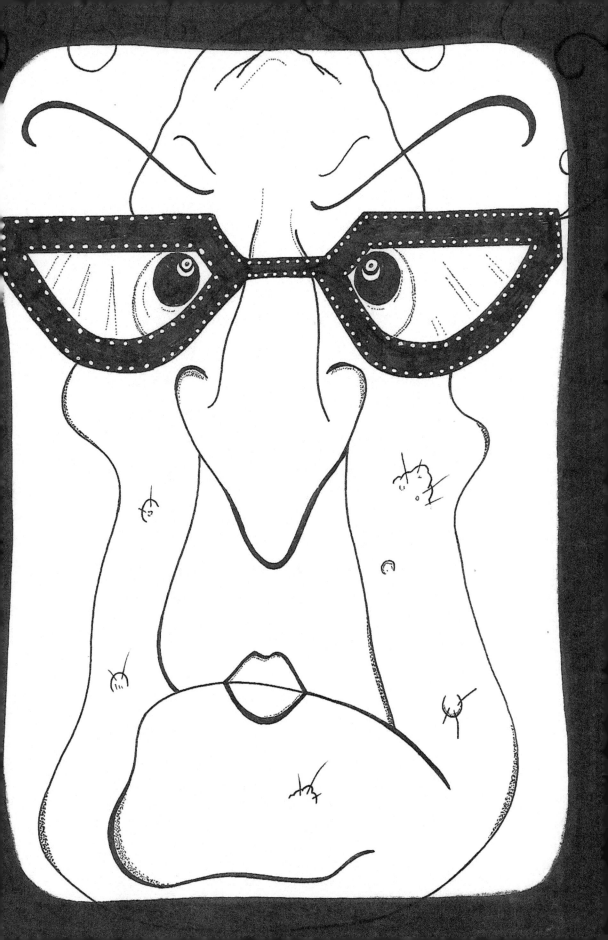

# WHAT'S A HOUSEWARMING PARTY?


A warming of a house, but why?
It needs no extra heat?
And will it poach or bake or fry?
What parts do people eat?


Who opens up the fiery door?
And will their skin start peeling?
Are burning coals on every floor,
with dragons on the ceiling?


I bet it's cos our house is newer,
they'll have to entertain.
And does it turn upon a skewer,
like hog roast on a flame?


I bet the wind is always banned.
Does steam leak through the walls?
Do people fly from arctic land,
to visit blazing halls?

Do locals bring in radiators,
and boiling kettles, too?
They'll need to carry aviators-
the sun's too close to view.

And does it funnel heat from space,
then cook upon a grill?
It's happy with a dripping face,
but never with the bill!

Hot water bottles on each bed?
do windows say, please shut?
Is silver foil wrapped round each head?
will people turn to soot?

I bet there's lava pools nearby,
and even ghosts will sweat?
"It's party time when people buy,
but never with, To Let."

## WHO'S DRIVING WHO?

I'm driving mummy up the wall.
She says this means she's cross!
But will she start, or simply stall,
I've got the keys! Who's boss?
And can I steer upon the roof
and leave her parked up there?
I guess I should've told the truth,
while sitting on the stair!
I see no wheels upon her side
or on her soles of feet.
Not eight feet long, or six feet wide,
nor parked upon the street!
And is she diesel, petrol too,
electric, fairy dust?
I made myself a mischief stew,
then sprinkled with mistrust.
She must come down, she's turning red,
she's upside down, you see.
That rush of blood to mummy's head
will surely spoil her tea!

# DON'T SHAKE YOUR HEAD!

The land of nod is what it's called.
I never move my head!

Does this affect all dreams installed
while fast asleep in bed?

Will dreams turn sour if I should stop
and shake the other way?

Will sheep still skip, and jump, and hop,
through lands of come-what-may?

# IF ONE SHOULD SQUINT THEIR EYES

I run inside the hamster wheel,
then tightrope on a hair.
I skid across banana peel,
then stumble down each stair!

I maypole round a drawing pin;
no keyhole is too small.
I think you've guessed, I'm young and thin--
and millimetres tall!

# I'LL HAVE IT WHOLE

"It's a piece of cake," I heard them say,
which means it's simple, yes.
No stresses, troubles, on the way--
what's on the menu? Guess!
Now, hop aboard, all chefs, all cooks;
I'll sample every slice.
Please make the ones I see in books,
draw lines through every price.
The seven tier will start me off,
the cherry topped with plum.
No preference to what I'll scoff,
just keep it hush from mum!
Banoffee pie upon my plate,
then carrot with no frosting.
Strawberry, lemon, figs and date,
confirm there's zero costing?
Vanilla topped with apples, pears,
a slab of cloud with sky;
two rainbow cakes with cosmic layers,
it's try but never buy!

But stars won't scatter from a sieve;
not all's a piece of cake.
If one should take more than you give,
you've baked a big mistake...

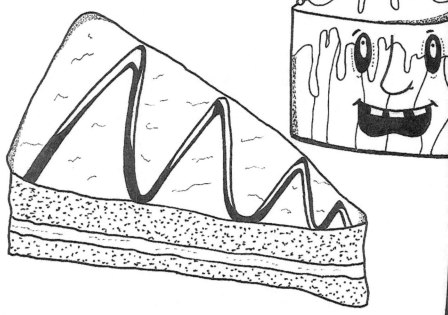

# DRIVEN BY MUSIC

It's not electric, there's no plug;
it ain't a solar brand.
It's taken five to lift, then tug--
that's why they call them grand.
If you should lift the lid, you'll see
no silver wire inside.
I wonder if it needs a key
to take it for a ride?
I see an engine--many parts--
but where's the steering wheel?
You press the keys, and then it starts
and moves to how you feel...
The pedals are not like they said,
and when my feet press on,
I'm rising higher than my bed.
I played its favourite song!
I'm through the roof, with unknown cause,
but how's my chair afloat?
I carry on, throughout applause
while striking many notes!
And now, I think, I must return
from grand piano dream.
My fingertips begin to burn,
and, through each key, there's steam...

# A CASE OF FURRY WEATHER

I see the whiskers fall from high,
I take this as a warning.
Torrential rain, from rumbling sky,
will soon begin its pouring.

I hear the clangs of bells, at first;
there's bowls of milk, and treats.
You think you'd see them at their worst,
piled high upon the streets.

Some try to land with style and sass--
a poodle sniffs a Persian.
No windscreen wiper cleans the glass
when rain's a different version.

They bounce back up, no cuts, no bruise,
there's no need for a brolly.
Spaniels, dachshunds, cockapoos,
a Great Dane and a collie.

Within the crowd, there's Siamese.
The weatherman was wrong.
A tabby blows amidst the breeze,
a Bengal meows a song.

It's rare to see the K9's here,
let loose from lawful cloud.
They try to make the weather clear...
but know it's not allowed!

At least I'm dry, not cold and wet.
The skies are never plain.
No need to shelter, don't forget--
when cats and dogs are rain!

## POTATO PANIC!

You see, my skin's so coarse and

tough, I always use concealer.

But what's the point in looking buff

When meeting Mr Peeler...

## UNRAVEL THE MUMMY

They want to see what lies inside,

like bones, and guts, and hair...

He's eight foot tall and two feet wide,

But only made of air!

## A SLOW DOWNPOUR

I watch each flake fall down so slow,

in simple downward routes.

Is snow just rain in fluffy coats

attached on parachutes?

# MRS ALLERGY HAS NO APOLOGY!

Her name is Dry, her nickname,
roasted. She's made of nuts, you see.
Who's guessed her middle name is
Salted? Her surname is KP...
And when she'd sneeze she'd say
'Cashew', then advertise the pine.
The Almond ones she likes to chew...
renaming them as, 'mine'.
She loves to eat pistachio
and recommends the chest.
She says she's from Brazil, you know;
the ones that crack are best.
A lifelong peanut butter fan,
the crunchy kind will soothe.
But when she's starved, a change of
plan, she'll munch upon the smooth.
Hickory ones do not belong
in dickery dock, the rhyme.
Mrs Allergy does you wrong.
I'll teach you anytime...

# OH, WHERE'S THE VOICE?

Whoever's put my voice on mute?
I call you now, a thief.
I'll search the house and every route,
and upturn every leaf.
I'll shake the worms beneath the rose.
It's playing hide and seek!
I'll check between the giant's toes;
I've heard he sleeps all week.
And what about the dentists, too,
they open every mouth.
I'll even go to Timbuktu,
then travel further South.
And does it hover like the fog,
or skip right through the rain?
It's not inside the chocolate log
or in the Lion's mane.
I look within the microwave,
unplatting all my hair.
There's echoes in the forest cave,
I wonder if it's there?

I'll check the Jack inside the box;
it could be trapped a while.
I'll even check all daddy's socks,
although the smells are vile.
It could be down the toilet bend--
whoever would have flushed?
I hope I don't set off a trend,
so everyone is hushed?
I check this sealed envelope,
and in the tumble dryer.
I search the moon with telescope,
but cannot get much higher.
The spider's web has just been plucked,
to see if it falls out.
There's not a place I haven't looked;
I really musn't shout!
And just how long will I remain
All tender, sore, and hoarse?
My daddy whispers, I'll explain...
let nature take its course!

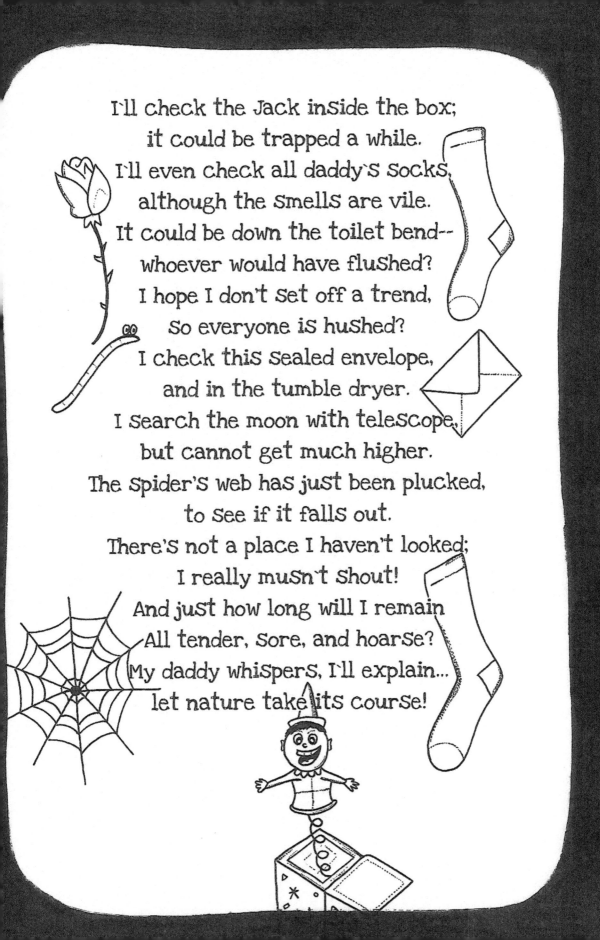

# IT'S RATHER COLD!

There's never sun, no birds, no bees.
Too cold for me, or you.
He'll never sneeze an antifreeze,
and all his bones are blue.

Nitrogen's his favourite drink,
His enemy, the heat.
He sleeps upon a skating rink
and dreams of snow and sleet.

And all his veins are icicles
That never pump what's warm.
His diet's never practical;
his nickname's winter storm.

He doesn't like the igloo much.
His skin is made of frost.
He'll fly away from summer's touch,
regardless of the cost...

## A SPRINKLE OF WHAT?

They say my food needs seasoning.

I'm not sure what that means.

Winter, autumn, summer, spring--

upon my chips and beans?

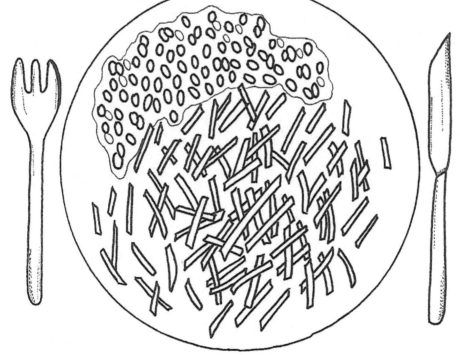

# DIALLING THE SUN

4

I cannot ring the sun to hear
its funny, cosmic tone.

Although, at times it looks quite near,
I simply cannot phone!

The sundial works when skies are bold
and rays are in their prime.

'It's not that kind of dial", I'm told--
It's there to tell the time!

# WHO'S THAT A-KNOCKING?

I'll turn into a leprechaun
and knock upon your door.
I'll wake you up with klaxon horn,
then stamp upon your floor.

I'll carry moonbeams on my back
and rays of sun in jars.
I'll stuff the rainbow in a sack,
then smuggle all the stars.

I'll pile my coins; they'll skim the roof.
Then you may knock them over.
For those who doubt, I'll leave them proof.
My hat, with four leaf clover.

If nobody believes the hype
of fairy tales, fantastic.
The DNA within my pipe
will prove my myth. My magic.

## MR FLEXIBLE

He stands upon his head, for show,
to always entertain.

Just watch how wide his legs can go;
he never speaks of pain.

His stretchy legs will reach so high,
a human seesaw, see.

But only if you reach the sky
can you get on for free!

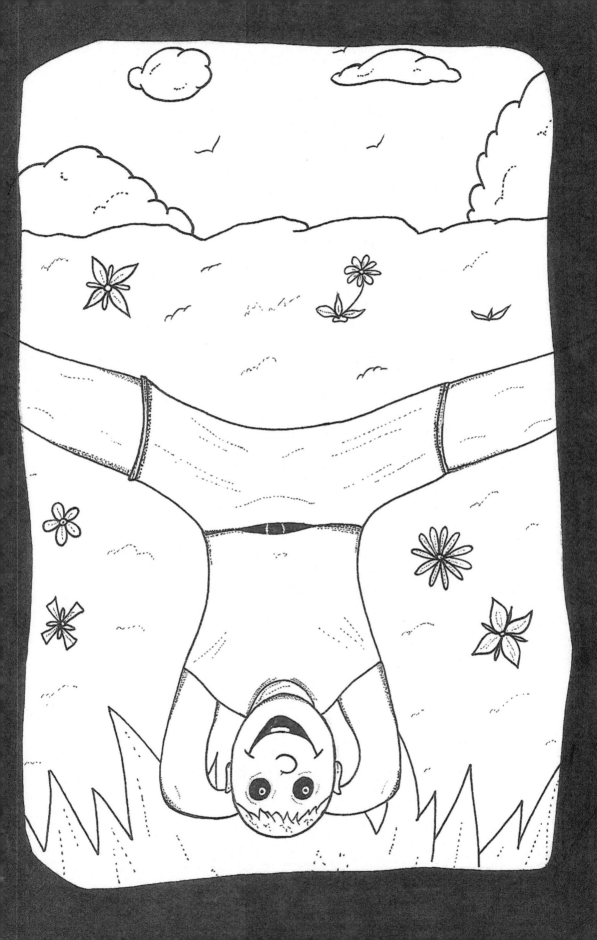

# EMERICAN ANGLISH

It's true that what I call a boot
is called a trunk afar--
within each state, through every route,
on every single car.

Their postal system's known as zip,
but we can't fasten these?
Who's brand new sneakers look more hip?
They're trainers, if you please!

With different rules, and many codes,
they call them sidewalks: why?
'Cos pavements that adjoin their
roads have people passing by.

The dime and pound, nickel and
pence, dollar and the fiver.
At times some words may make no
sense, like nappy and the diaper.

The Z and S are troublesome,
when reading different books.
They call it fanny, we say bum.
If something's bad, it sucks.
The eggplant and the aubergine
can cause confusion here.
'Cos I can't scramble, fry, or poach--
I've tried, yet persevere!
I love the cooling autumn breeze.
It's summer's curtain call.
With pumpkins carved for Hallows Eve,
their season's known as 'fall.'
I've looked outside the window pane,
to view the weather, clear.
'Cos someone asked to check the rain,
not sure what that means here?
So, there's some education,
free; such things are all the same.
I see no need to disagree.
They're just a different name!

# CHEESE IF YOU PLEASE?

I dream of cheese, in every form.
I'll never get enough,
though some are savoured cold or warm,
and some are smooth, or rough.
It's like a mini fashion show,
they gather round, all shapes.
Some battle over who should go
to sit among the grapes.
The cocktail sticks are nearby,
my bread is now their mattress.
The gorgonzola says, "Goodbye."
its smell's too bad for business.
The camembert has thickish skin,
so never gets upset.
I try a slice of stilton, thin,
but much to my regret!

# PINS AND NEEDLES

The pins aren't from my bedroom wall,
I feel them 'neath my knees.
The needles can't sow mummy's shawl
or stitch shalwar kameez.

They're never bought from textile store,
yet always cause me strain.
I've sat for hours upon this floor--
a self-inflicted pain!

'Cos, when I walk, my legs feel strange;
I try to move, then kick.
Can't take them off to rearrange--
when pins and needles prick.

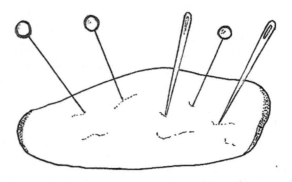

# YOU'VE GOT A NERVE!

Today, I banged my funny bone,
but why's it have to ache?
It made me shout, and curse, and moan;
its name's a big mistake...

It doesn't grin each time I poke
or have a laughing fit.
I've never heard it tell a joke
or giggle when it's hit.

The elbow's such a random place,
I prod it and observe.
It's not a bone, in any case--
it's just a little nerve!

HA

HA

HA-HA!

HA

HA-HA!

He thinks my behaviour's petty;

I guess he could be right.

I swapped his laces with spaghetti;

he couldn't pull them tight!

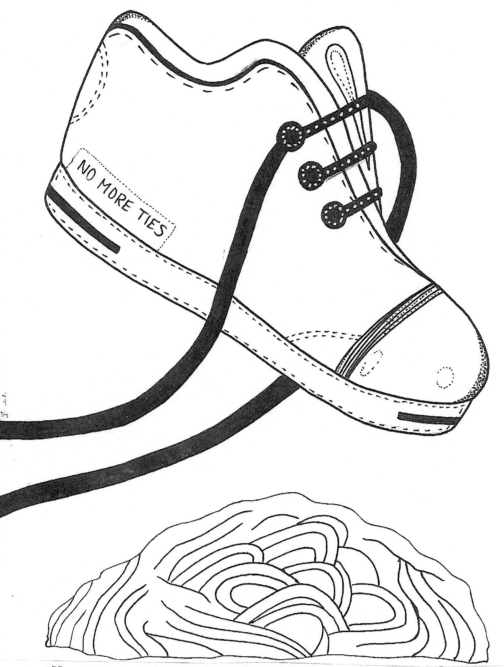

All poems are written by Elliot Chester. Some images drawn are from the public domain and are free to use.

Printed in Great Britain
by Amazon